Adam's Alternative Sports Day

of related interest

Can I tell you about Asperger Syndrome?
A Guide for Friends and Family
Jude Welton
Illustrated by Jane Telford
ISBN 1 84310 206 4

What did you say? What do you mean?
An illustrated guide to understanding metaphors
Jude Welton
Illustrated by Jane Telford
ISBN 1 84310 207 2

Blue Bottle Mystery
An Asperger Adventure
Kathy Hoopmann
ISBN 1 85302 978 5

Of Mice and Aliens
An Asperger Adventure
Kathy Hoopmann
ISBN 1 84310 007 X

Lisa and the Lacemaker
An Asperger Adventure
Kathy Hoopmann
ISBN 1 84310 071 1

Buster and the Amazing Daisy
Nancy Ogaz
ISBN 1 84310 721 X

Mind Reading
The Interactive Guide to Emotions
Based on research by Cambridge University, led by Simon Baron-Cohen
DVD-ROM ISBN 1 84310 214 5
CD-ROM set ISBN 1 84310 215 3

Adam's Alternative Sports Day

An Asperger Story

Jude Welton

Jessica Kingsley Publishers
London and Philadelphia

First published in 2005
by Jessica Kingsley Publishers
116 Pentonville Road
London N1 9JB, UK
and
400 Market Street, Suite 400
Philadelphia, PA 19106, USA

www.jkp.com

Copyright © Jude Welton 2005

Library of Congress Cataloging in Publication Data
A CIP catalog record for this book is available from the Library of Congress

British Library Cataloguing in Publication Data
A CIP catalogue record for this book is available from the British Library

ISBN-13: 978 1 84310 300 4
ISBN-10: 1 84310 300 1

Printed and Bound in Great Britain by
Athenaeum Press, Gateshead, Tyne and Wear

To JJ and Charlotte

Acknowledgements

Social Stories and comic strip conversations are referred to in the story – these useful techniques for sharing social information were devised by Carol Gray. I'd like to say a big thank you to Carol Gray, and to the following people for taking the time to read the manuscript of *Adam's Alternative Sports Day* and comment on it before publication: Sue Churchill, Eileen Griffith, Robert Jones, Elizabeth Newson – and as always, David and JJ. Thanks also to JJ for the drawings on pages 61 and 62.

Contents

Dear Reader

I hope you will enjoy reading about Adam and his friends, and the challenges they face.

If you'd like to, please have a go at the challenges yourself, and try to crack the hieroglyphic code and the riddles. If the solutions are visible, there will be a warning telling you to cover up the appropriate page.

Chapter 1

PE on a Tuesday!

Adam took a deep breath, held it, and started to count silently, inside his head – 1...2...3...4...5. Then he let his breath out slowly.

"Another breath in, hold it – 1...2...3...4...5 – breathe out," he thought. He told himself, remembering to tell himself silently, inside his head, not saying it aloud, that he was relaxed. He could cope with anything.

The school door opened, and the noise of the queue got louder as everyone pushed to get through the door. Adam held back, waiting until there was a quiet gap to get through without being crushed.

Soon he was at his peg. He knew where his peg was. It was right at the end, down the quietest bit of the corridor. It gave him space to unpack his bag without anyone bumping into him. He liked that.

Adam glanced at the checklist above his peg. He hung up his coat and rucksack, took out his folder, his reading book (*The Ultimate History of Cars*) and his snack. Carefully balancing his snack on top of his book, and his book on his folder, he made his way slowly to the classroom.

His teacher, Mrs White, always wrote the day's timetable on the blackboard so that she and the children could keep track of what was happening when. Adam was glad. It made him feel safe. Adam didn't like surprises or uncertainties. If he didn't know what was going to happen, he would start to feel panicky.

Like last week when Mrs White was ill, and a new supply teacher came in for the day. She was very friendly, but she did all the wrong things. First of all she came in and said, "Hello everyone. My name is Mrs Best. I'm afraid Mrs White is ill."

("Why is she afraid of that?" Adam had thought. "Should we be afraid too?")

"So," Mrs Best continued, "Today will be different from usual."

("Oh no," thought Adam. He hated "different".)

"Today will be a day for surprises."(Adam felt his hands go sweaty. He stuck his finger nails into his palms.)

"It's a lovely sunny day, so after registration we'll go outside for PE."

("But it's Tuesday morning," thought Adam, increasingly worried. "We do PE on Thursday afternoon.")

Adam didn't like PE anyway, especially with a teacher he didn't know. But he was used to doing PE on Thursday afternoons, with Mrs White. He knew what to expect, and she always explained things to him carefully.

Mrs Best was smiling and speaking, but Adam wasn't hearing what she said. He was starting to panic. His friend

Josie recognized the signs. He'd gone very pale and his mouth was tensed up. Josie touched his shoulder. "Do you feel all right Adam?"

Adam could feel tears coming. He felt angry with himself. He didn't want to cry. "No," said Adam, "I'm worried. I don't want to do PE. I want to go home."

Just then, the door opened, and the headteacher, Mr Williams came in. He asked to have a word with Mrs Best. "Open your reading books everybody," he said, "and read quietly until Mrs Best comes back. We'll just be a few minutes."

He looked over at Adam and said, "Adam, will you come out into the corridor please."

Adam got up from his desk, and went over to Mr Williams, who put his hands on Adam's shoulders and said, "You go and sit in the reading corner, Adam, while I have a quick word with Mrs Best. You can get yourself a drink of water first if you like."

Adam had begun to feel less panicky as soon as he felt Mr Williams touch his shoulder. He poured himself a drink from the water machine and drank it slowly. It tasted cool and good. He went to the beanbag in the reading corner and closed his eyes. He took a deep breath in – 1...2...3...4...5 – and then let his breath out slowly.

When he opened his eyes, he could see Mr Williams and Mrs Best walking towards him down the corridor. "Adam," said Mr Williams, "I've just been talking to Mrs Best. I wasn't at school first thing this morning, so I wasn't able to speak to her earlier. But it's all right. Now Mrs Best knows you have Asperger Syndrome, Adam. She's taught another child with AS, so she understands. Are you ready to go back to class now?"

Adam was ready. He went back in and sat down next to Josie. Mrs Best followed. This time she began by writing the day's timetable on the blackboard. Adam gave a sigh of relief when he saw that PE wasn't on the list after all.

Chapter 2

The Tortoise and the Hare

That was last week. Today was Wednesday. Wednesday 4th of June. Two weeks and two days before Sports Day. Every year, as Sports Day approached, Adam counted the days. He dreaded Sports Day. He dreaded coming last. He dreaded the disappointment of not being chosen for any of the team events. He just dreaded it.

Today's first session was ERIC, Everyone Reading In Class. Adam started reading his Cars book. He turned to his favourite page, and read:

Subaru Impreza
Engines: 1.6 or 2.0 litre petrol
Body styles: 4-door saloon, 5-door hatchback
Dimensions: 4.41m x 1.70m
Prices: £13,770 (1.6TS) to £27,810 (2.0 WRX
Sti Performance Pk)

Next to him, his friend Josie was reading a story about horses. Across the table, the new boy, James, was looking at his football magazine, and Anita was reading a book of funny poems about animals with silly names.

After ERIC was Computer Work, Adam's favourite. He sometimes wished that all his work could be done on computer. Computers were so predictable. When you keyed in something, you knew what to expect. And they were fun. And they made sense.

As usual, Adam finished his computer work first, and was then able to help the ones who found it more difficult. He loved helping them. It felt good to be able to do things well.

Once Mrs Forest, who came into school sometimes to work with him in the quiet room, had asked him to make lists of what made him feel good about himself, and what made him feel bad about himself. Being good at computers and being able to help others with their computer work were at the top of his first list. Adam's "What makes me feel good about myself" list is on the opposite page.

The list of things that made him feel bad felt a lot, lot longer. In fact, it wasn't any longer. It just felt it. Turn the page to see Adam's "What makes me feel bad about myself" list.

What makes me feel good about myself

1. Being good with computers.

2. Helping others with their computer work.

3. Being good at maths.

4. Being good at chess.

5. Swimming fast.

6. Having a good memory.

7. Knowing a lot about cars and dinosaurs and Egypt.

8. Playing with Josie.

9. Being asked round to someone's house to play.

10. Getting stickers for good work. (I got 8 last term, and 7 the term before that. The year before, I got 24 altogether, which was 2 more than Josie!)

What makes me feel bad about myself

1. Making mistakes.

2. Getting muddled up about what I'm supposed to do to get organized.

3. Getting worried about things.

4. Finding loud noises difficult to cope with.

5. Finding changes of plan difficult to cope with.

6. Wanting to go on sleepovers, but sometimes being too worried to do it.

7. Not enjoying birthday parties. (Too many people. Too much noise. Not winning games. Singing the birthday song, which I don't like at all.)

8. Not being good at football. (It all goes so fast, and if I do get the ball I usually don't know who to kick it to. If I do know who to kick it to, it never seems to go where I want.)

9. Not being chosen for the football team.

10. Being the only person I know with Asperger Syndrome.

Unlike Computer Work, lunchtime was not a favourite with Adam. Mainly because of no. 4 on his second list. During his first term at the school, he had sat in the lunch hall with his fingers stuck in his ears to block out the noise. The 143 children all **SCRAPING** their chairs on the wooden floor, **CLASHING** their knives, forks and plates, and talking so loudly. Now he was getting used to the noise, but when he had finished his lunch, he mostly went to spend a few minutes quiet time down by the trees at the bottom of the school field.

Here he could run around by himself, telling himself stories of his adventures in Egypt, discovering hidden tombs, cracking hieroglyphic codes that led to golden treasures. Sometimes his friend Josie joined in his ancient Egypt adventures. At other times, they acted out medieval stories. Then, Adam was Damar, a brave warrior, and Josie was Josay, an elf princess.

Josie usually waited for a little while before she joined him and asked him if he wanted to play. She knew he needed his time by himself. Her cousin Tom had AS too. So she understood when Mrs White had explained to the class last year that Adam had Asperger Syndrome, and explained how it meant that Adam had lots of talents, but had some difficulties too, mainly with what she called "social sense" but also with "motor skills".

Josie had thought that every nine-year-old would have difficulties driving a car, but Mrs White explained that "motor skills" had a special meaning and that it meant that Adam had some problems with body movements, which could make things like sport a bit difficult for him. Mrs

White also explained that Adam had problems dealing with loud noises. Tom didn't have that problem, but he hated bright flashing lights.

Mrs White also said that Adam had special interests. He was really into Egypt, and cars and computers. Josie didn't see at first why this was unusual. Everyone had special interests. Her big love was horses. She always spent her pocket money on a horse magazine, and still enjoyed all her horse models she'd had since she was little. While Adam drew hieroglyphs and pictures of cars, she drew horses.

But as Josie got to know Adam better, she realized that he often wanted to **only** talk about Egypt or tell her **lots** of facts about cars. Sometimes she had to remind him not to go on and on about cars. "Five more car facts, Adam," she'd say, "and then let's change the subject."

Adam often wasn't happy about changing the subject, particularly if he was stressed out. But he usually managed it, especially when they got into one of their fantasy adventure games.

This Wednesday lunchtime, as usual, Josie ran over to where Adam was playing. "Hi Adam." she said, "What are you playing? Can we play together?"

"Yes, we can. I'm planning an adventure in Egypt," said Adam. "We've got to find our way to a hidden tomb. The clues are hidden in hieroglyphs. Then we have to go through a series of challenges."

"Great," said Josie. She loved playing this game.

When the bell rang for the end of lunch break, Adam and Josie joined the others in the school hall for Assembly. Adam watched Mr Williams as he came onto the stage in the school hall. He liked his headteacher. He had a calm voice and spoke slowly. Just the sort of way Adam wished everyone would speak.

(Adam had been to an after-school group once, but didn't go a second time. The group leader had a loud, harsh voice, and he spoke in a snappy way as if he was always angry. He spoke quickly too, and made Adam feel muddled.)

"Good afternoon everybody," smiled Mr Williams.

"Good **afternoon Mis**ter **Will**iams," the school chanted back in a slow rhythm. Adam liked this little routine.

"All of you should have found an envelope on your seat. Has everyone got one?" A murmur of yesses went through the crowd.

"Good," said Mr Williams. "Don't open it or look at it yet. I want you to listen to a story first. Today I'm going to tell you a story that many of you will know already. It's one of Aesop's fables. It's the story of the Tortoise and the Hare.

"The Tortoise and the Hare are going to have a race. The Hare knows that he is much, much faster than the Tortoise, and can easily win. They set off together, and sure enough, the Hare speeds ahead.

"The Hare is fast, but also a bit lazy – and over-confident. He thinks to himself 'The Tortoise must be ages behind me. I've got time for a sit down and a rest.' So he sits down in the shade of a tree. He closes his eyes…and falls asleep. Meanwhile, as the Hare snoozes, the Tortoise keeps plodding on. After a while, he reaches the Hare and passes him. By the time the Hare wakes up from his sleep, the Tortoise has reached the finishing post!

"Now the moral of this fable is SLOW AND STEADY WINS THE RACE. That's one moral we can learn from it. But when I was thinking about Sports Day, Aesop's story started me thinking about what it means to win a race.

"Aesop isn't actually saying that the slow and steady tortoise would win the 100 metres or the interhouse relay." (Giggles in the audience.)

"Perhaps Aesop wanted us to not just think about winning races, but valuing different qualities. The tortoise is not just slow and steady. He plans ahead. He's aware of his own and the hare's strengths and weaknesses. These are important qualities – in a person as well as in a tortoise. (More giggles, some groans.) They are just as important as speed or sporting talent.

"Anyway, thinking about the tortoise and the hare made me rethink my ideas on Sports Day. As you all know, Sports Day is in two weeks."

("Two weeks and two days," thought Adam, despondently.)

"Well, this year," said Mr Williams, "I thought we would have an Alternative Sports Day. Rather than races, we will be setting you all a series of challenges during this week and next week. These challenges will test all sorts of skills and abilities. Then the seven children – one from each year – who have earned the most points during the challenges will be chosen as class champions to compete on the Alternative Sports Day."

Adam, who usually hated changes of plan, was smiling to himself. He could hardly believe what he was hearing. A different kind of Sports Day. No coming last in the races. No not being chosen for the relay team.

"This must be what people mean when they say 'It's like a dream come true'."

Chapter 3

Alternative Sports Day

"The final seven won't compete against each other," continued Mr Williams. "The idea is to work *together* as a team to find a set of hidden treasures."

Mr Williams stopped talking and looked around.

"Is everyone clear? Right. Now, please open your envelopes and take a look at the sheet of paper that was on your chair. This will explain what I've just said in a bit more detail."

Adam read his sheet of paper.

ALTERNATIVE SPORTS

Thursday June 5	HIEROGLYPHIC CODE
Friday June 6	MENTAL MATHS
Monday June 9	RIDDLE
Tuesday June 10	JIGSAW
Wednesday June 11	CLASS QUIZ
Thursday June 12	NO CHALLENGES
Friday June 13	WRITING
Monday June 16	RESULTS. CHOOSING CLASS CHAMPIONS
Tuesday June 17	NO CHALLENGES
Wednesday June 18	NO CHALLENGES
Thursday June 19	NO CHALLENGES
Friday June 20	CLASS CHAMPIONS CHALLENGES

When Adam's mum picked him up from the school gate that afternoon, she didn't find the usual pale- faced, tense-looking child. Instead, Adam was smiling broadly and grasping his piece of paper in his hand.

"Guess what, Mum?" he said. "There's no Sports Day."

"Thank goodness," she thought to herself. She and Adam's Dad dreaded Sports Day as much as Adam did. She hadn't known one that hadn't ended in tears. But since she had never told Adam this, she just said casually, "Why not?"

"Well, Mr Williams told us about the Tortoise and the Hare. And he said that speed and sporting talent aren't the only important things. So instead of our usual Sports Day, we are going to have a series of challenges, testing all sorts of things. Quizzes and maths and puzzles and all that."

"That sounds great," said Adam's mum, as they walked towards the car. "They are the sorts of things you like, aren't they?"

"Yes they are. And do you know what the first challenge is? Look here," he said, pushing the piece of paper into her hand. "Read it out."

"You read it to me."

"No, you read it. I want to hear you read it." (Adam often liked to hear her read something aloud to him, even if he knew what he was going to hear.)

"Hieroglyphic code," read Adam's mum. "Adam, that's great. Just your thing."

"I might get picked to be the champion from my class, Mum, and be in the final seven." Adam was getting very excited.

"That would be wonderful, love, but it doesn't matter if you're not." She was trying to prepare him for disappointment. When Adam wanted something, he wanted it so much and he thought about it so intensely that he was almost bound to be disappointed.

"Still," she allowed herself to think, "he's got more chance than he ever has had. Wouldn't it be great?" She imagined a lovely picture in her head. Adam. Her son. Holding the Challenge Cup, with a huge, beaming smile. She didn't know it, but Adam was having exactly the same thought.

Chapter 4

Adam and the Hieroglyphs

That evening Adam spent hours reading his books on Ancient Egypt. He was so excited that he couldn't get to sleep until his CD had played his favourite album through twice. So he was tired the next morning, but he couldn't wait to get to school.

As he entered the classroom he saw the timetable Mrs White had written up on the blackboard. First thing was HIEROGLYPHS. Mrs White handed out a sheet of paper, with a key to the hieroglyphs along the top and a hieroglyphic message below.

"Quiet please, everyone," she said. "Now I want you to work individually on this code. For some of the other challenges, you will work in teams. But this first one is for you each to do by yourself. And no cheating please! I shall be watching carefully. Any questions? Ready? You may start now."

The shuffling of paper sounded throughout the class. Some faces looked excited and keen. Some looked bewildered. But Adam didn't notice. He felt a fluttering of excitement and determination inside him. Often in class, especially if he didn't like the subject or found it difficult, he couldn't focus on what he was doing. Now all he could see and think about was the hieroglyphic code. Look on the next page to see what was on the piece of paper.

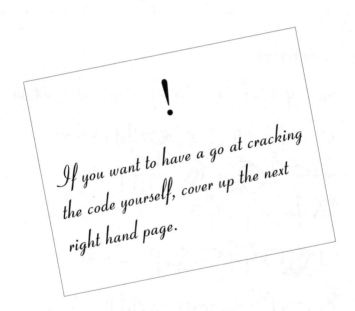

!

If you want to have a go at cracking the code yourself, cover up the next right hand page.

KEY TO HIEROGLYPHS

A	D	E	F	H	I

K	M	N	O	P	R

S	T	U	W	Y	Z

CRACK THE CODE

Adam started to go systematically through the key at the top of the page. He was familiar with the hieroglyph symbols, but he knew there were lots of slightly different versions. So he checked carefully, memorizing the equivalent letters and pictures. It was confusing, as some of the English letters, such as e and y, and u and w, had the same hieroglyphs. He had to work out what made sense.

FIRST TO FIND THE HIDDEN TRYA...

("No, that can't be right," he thought.)

...TREA...SURE...WINS IT

This was just like the game he and Josie played with each other. He let his attention slip for a few seconds. "I wonder how Josie is doing?" he thought. He looked across the table to where Josie was bent over her sheet of paper, elbow shielding her answers from James' view. Josie didn't trust James, especially since he copied her spellings last week. Josie was very good at spelling. And hieroglyphs. And riddles.

"Oh no," thought Adam, "Josie's going to beat me!" And then he thought, "Oh dear, how long have I been thinking about what Josie is doing? I've got to focus." He looked back at his paper. Suddenly, what had all seemed so clear looked muddled and the letters and pictures didn't make sense. Adam felt himself panic. "Calm down," he told himself silently, "Breathe deeply and start again."

It worked. He'd got himself back into focus, and within a few seconds he had the first word of the next section.

PAPERWS

("No, that's not right."

...PAPY...PAPYRUS.

And then the next few.

IN MRS WHITES

"In Mrs White's what?" thought Adam, as he copied down the letters.

D...E...S...K...DRAWER

Adam jumped up and started to walk quickly over towards Mrs White's desk. As he did so, he knocked over a chair and bent down to pick it up again.
By the time he had put it back into its place, Josie and James had also left their seats. Adam knew it was against the rules to run in class. He tried to walk as quickly as he could. He could see James trying to elbow Josie out of the way, so that he could walk in front of her. Who would get to the desk first?

Chapter 5

The Nasty Smile

All three arrived at Mrs White's desk together. They looked at each other. Then Adam and Josie looked at Mrs White.

"What shall we do?" asked Adam, his voice high and panicky.

James didn't wait to hear the reply. He grabbed the drawer handle, pulled open the drawer and took out a roll of heavy paper, which had been made to look like an ancient scroll of papyrus. James opened it up. Adam was standing right next to him, and could read what it said.

CONGRATULATIONS
You have won
the first
challenge!

Adam felt his face going red, and his eyes getting hot as they filled with tears. "It's not fair," he thought. "I was first to crack the code. If I hadn't gone back to pick up that chair, I would be holding the papyrus. I would be the winner."

Adam could feel disappointment and anger starting to rumble like thunder inside him. He struggled to stop himself from crying, and from grabbing the papyrus from James. James had told Adam that he always came first in Sports Day races. Adam had noticed that he didn't usually have the same success in class.

"Perhaps Josie didn't hide her page from him well enough," thought Adam.

Luckily, Mrs White soon spoke. "Well, well, well," she smiled. "It looks as if we have three winners to the first challenge. You all arrived at my desk at the same time. Well done. Now if you go back to your seats, I'll take the papyrus and get two more made, so all three of you will have one."

As Adam made his way back to his seat, he watched what looked like a swimming sea of faces, and heard the loud applause echoing in his ears. The children clapped and clapped until he, Josie and James all sat back down at the same table.

"Quiet now, everybody," said Mrs White, raising her hand for silence. Everyone stopped talking. The silence was a welcome relief to Adam, but still he felt flustered and over-excited. "Well done everyone. And particularly to James, Adam and Josie. Your table was very successful."

"Our table?" thought Adam. "Our table didn't have anything to do with it," he said to Josie.

"She means that all the winners came from this table." Josie whispered her reply.

"Oh," said Adam. "I wish she'd say what she meant."

At break time, Adam and Josie sat on a bench in the far corner of the school playing fields, sharing their snacks. It was a warm, calm morning, and Adam felt warm and calm too. He and Josie hadn't said much after Mrs White had announced that they were joint winners. They sat without talking and crunched contentedly on their crisps as they watched a group of boys playing football nearby.

Most of the boys were in the top class, a year older than Adam and Josie, but James was with them. Someone kicked the ball over towards the bench. Adam jumped up and went to kick the ball back to them. And missed.

James ran up smiling. Adam wondered if this was a "nice smile" or a "nasty smile", like the one Uncle Vernon once gave Harry Potter when they first went to King's Cross Station in *Harry Potter and the Philosopher's Stone.* When Mum had read this to him the year before last, he had asked how a smile could be nasty. He thought smiles were supposed to be a sign of friendliness or happiness.

Mum had explained that usually a smile showed that a person was happy or being friendly. But sometimes people might smile and not be happy **or** friendly. Sometimes people used the expressions on their faces to hide what they really felt for some reason. Like a kind of trick. And sometimes they might smile because they were taking pleasure in thinking about something nasty happening to the person they were with – if they didn't like them, or they had had an argument. A smile could mean so many things! And how could you tell which? Why was it all so complicated?

When Adam worked with Mrs Forest, they sometimes looked at pictures of faces. First, she had drawn cartoons with smiley faces for "happy", and an upside down smile for "sad". But Adam thought they looked nothing like happy and sad faces. He had looked in the mirror and tried to make his mouth go into an upside-down smile, but it wouldn't.

Later, they had looked at faces on a CD-ROM, and Adam had to select an "emotion" from a list and match the emotion with the expression. Adam thought this was much better, as there were photos and video clips of real faces. He soon started making correct guesses and getting high scores, and that made him feel good.

As he looked at James, Adam ran through the CD-ROM images in his head, and compared them with the expression on James's face. He decided that James's smile was probably a "nasty smile". James's lips were turned upwards and his teeth were showing, but his eyes seemed to match someone's in the "sneaky" emotion group on the CD-ROM; someone who was demonstrating looking "insincere". (Mrs Forest had told him that when someone was being insincere, they were pretending to think or feel something that they weren't really thinking or feeling.)

When James spoke, Adam realized, with a tremor of triumph, that he was right. It was a **nasty** smile. Almost immediately, the sense of triumph was overtaken by hurt, anger and frustration.

"Missed the ball, did you, Adam?" said James. "Pity you're so clumsy. You'd have got to Mrs White's desk first if you hadn't knocked over that chair. Thought you'd won, didn't you? Just because you're always going on about Egypt and stuff."

Adam felt his face get hot, and felt the anger and frustration rising in him again. Before he could speak, Josie did. "You probably only got the answer because you cheated, James," she said angrily. "I saw you looking at what I was writing."

Before James could reply, one of the older boys came up to the group. Adam was relieved to see that it was Robert, the head of his house. He was always kind to Adam.

"Hurry up, James. Are you OK, Adam? What's the matter?" asked Robert.

"I'm OK," said Adam. "It's just that I tried to kick the ball back, and…"

"And missed as usual," interrupted James, in what Adam recognized was a sarcastic tone. (He and Mrs Forest had done "tones of voice".)

"**You** can talk, James!" said Robert.

("What does he mean?" thought Adam. "Of course James can talk.")

"It was you who kicked the ball out of play in the first place," Robert continued.

Adam saw James's face go red.

"Here, Adam, have another go," said Robert as he put the ball a few metres in front of Adam. "Now keep looking at the ball as you run towards it. And then kick it over towards the goalposts."

Adam put his crisp packet down. He ran towards the ball, and kicked. This time his foot connected exactly as he'd wanted it to. He watched the ball arc upwards, and glide down to where the little group of footballers was standing, right next to the goal. He smiled. So did Robert and Josie. James didn't.

"Nice one, Adam," said Robert. "See you later. And don't let James worry you."

James said nothing, but ran back to the pitch after Robert. For the second time that break Adam felt a sense of triumph. This time it was more of a glow than a tremor.

Chapter 6

Maths Practice

Adam was looking forward to Friday's mental maths competition. Ever since he was very little, he'd been good with numbers, and he almost always did well with maths at school. Not always though. If he was upset or worried about something, or hadn't slept well and was feeling tired, or if he happened to find that particular bit of maths difficult, he sometimes found that he just couldn't focus and made mistakes. Then he would get very upset.

Being good at maths was one of the things that made him feel good about himself (no. 3 on his What makes me feel good about myself list), but making mistakes was no. 1 on the What makes me feel bad about myself list.

He spent Thursday evening practising maths questions on his computer. Times tables. Divisions. Percentages. Over and over again. He asked his Dad to write out a list of sums and test him. They sat on opposite sides of the kitchen table, Dad reading out the questions and Adam bending over his paper, writing down the answers until his fingers hurt from holding the pencil so tightly for so long. Later on, he sat in bed writing out maths questions and answers from a maths quiz book.

Then, he couldn't get to sleep. It was as if he couldn't switch off his brain. He wanted to turn it off, just like he'd turned off his computer, but it wouldn't turn off. He couldn't stop thinking about numbers and quizzes and the possibility of winning. He put his on calming down CD. He counted backwards from a hundred – ten times. But at midnight, he was still awake. He woke Mum up and asked her to read to him.

Mum wasn't usually in a good mood when she was woken by Adam on one of the nights when he couldn't sleep. But tonight, she agreed to read to him from *The Hobbit*. As she read, Adam had clear pictures in his head of Bilbo travelling along the road to Rivendell. He imagined he heard the sound of Gandalf's long cloak swish past him…

"Good morning Adam," said Mum. It was morning. He could see the sunlight slipping under the edges of the black-out curtains.

"It's Thursday," thought Adam.

"Good morning Mum. It's the maths quiz today."

"I know. I've let you lie in a bit because you were so late going to sleep last night. So you'll need to keep focused on getting ready. You get dressed while I make breakfast."

Five minutes later, when his mum came back to his bedroom, Adam was still sitting in bed. With a loud sigh, which Adam knew usually came before her voice started to sound angry, she left the room. Adam had asked her once what the sigh meant.

"Exasperation, Adam."

"What do you mean?" he'd asked.

"Look it up, Adam," she'd said as she quickly turned away.

A few minutes later, Mum came back in with a list:

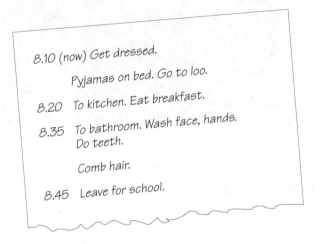

8.10 (now) Get dressed.

Pyjamas on bed. Go to loo.

8.20　To kitchen. Eat breakfast.

8.35　To bathroom. Wash face, hands.
Do teeth.

Comb hair.

8.45　Leave for school.

She had added a word at the bottom:

FOCUS!!

Adam and Mum arrived at the school gates just as the line of children was going in through the door. Adam walked quickly over to join the end of the line, took a deep breath, counted to five, breathed out slowly, and walked in.

When he got to his classroom, he looked up at the blackboard to see the day's timetable.

Friday 6 June

ERIC
Maths
Break
Language
Music
Lunch
Maths Quiz
Art with Mr Sims

Adam saw that he would have to wait until after lunch to do the maths quiz. He was so excited about it that he could hardly focus on his reading, even though it was his favourite car magazine.

In maths, Mrs White said she would give some practice for the afternoon's quiz. Everyone opened their exercise books, and got ready for the questions.

"15 minus 9."

6, wrote Adam quickly.

"Express 50 per cent as a fraction."

"½," thought Adam.

"9 multiplied by 7."

63, wrote Adam. He looked over to James, who was trying to see what Josie was writing. Josie had her arm bent protectively over her book, trying to stop him.

After 20 questions the quiz stopped, and Mrs White told everyone to swap exercise books with the person sitting next to them, for marking. Adam swapped with Anita, and Josie and James swapped too.

As Josie marked James's work, Adam heard her sigh. It sounded like the sigh that Mum made this morning. "Exasperation," he thought.

Adam was right. As Josie marked tick, tick, tick, tick, cross, tick, cross, tick, tick on James's exercise book, she recognized her own answers, correct and incorrect. She looked over at James and wondered what to do.

He had only been at the school for just over a week. When he first sat next to her, she had noticed that he was always looking at what she was writing, yet hiding his own work from her. At first she didn't mind. "He probably feels worried about not knowing how we do things," she had told herself.

Josie always tried to think the best of people, but she was starting to feel really angry with James. He never missed an opportunity to put her or Adam down. And he was a **cheat**. At first she thought it was just a coincidence that their answers were so alike, but now she was certain he was managing to see what she'd written.

She hated the idea of telling tales, but she made up her mind. She was definitely going to tell Mrs White about it. Maybe she should tell her at the end of the lesson, so that

Mrs White knew before they took the Mental Maths test. Maybe she should just write "copied" before the $^{16}/_{20}$ mark.

"Josie." Josie suddenly heard Mrs White's voice. "Josie. Please can you pass James back his exercise book."

As Adam watched Josie pass the book to James, he saw James smile. It was definitely a **nasty** smile, Adam thought.

Adam had scored $^{18}/_{20}$, while Anita, whose work he had marked, got $^{12}/_{20}$. Still, Adam was annoyed with himself for getting the last two questions wrong. He'd started to lose concentration at the end. "It was stupid," he said to himself. "I know that a quarter is 25 per cent, and that 8 multiplied by 12 is 96. Why did I get it wrong?"

Chapter 7

Learning to Lose

"Why did I get it wrong?" Adam was still repeating this to Josie when the bell rang for five minutes before the end of lunch break.

"Stop worrying about it, Adam. It doesn't matter," Josie said (for the eighth time). "Come on. I've got to rush. I want to catch Mrs White to tell her about James cheating. Will you come with me?"

"Why?" asked Adam.

"Because I'm scared."

When they arrived at the classroom, Mrs White was there already. But so was Mrs Thomas, James's mother. She was the new school secretary. Like James, she'd only just started at the school.

"Oh dear," said Josie, who had noticed that the two women had very serious expressions on their faces. "I can't tell her now."

"Why not?" asked Adam.

"Well, I can't tell Mrs White that James is cheating when his mum's standing there, can I?"

"Why not? He **is** cheating."

"Yes, but think about it, Adam. Think how Mrs Thomas would feel. She'd be so embarrassed, and so would Mrs White. And so would I."

Adam thought about it. But he had no idea how any of them would feel.

Just then, the rest of the class arrived, and Adam and Josie were pushed in through the door. He hated being pushed like this, and quickly stepped sideways, to allow the rush of children past.

When the others were at their seats, he went to sit down at his. He looked up to see Mrs White closing the door behind Mrs Thomas. Standing at her desk, Mrs White lifted her hand for silence. Everyone was quiet. "Well, it's time for the second challenge. The maths quiz. Now before we do this, we are going to have to rearrange the seating."

("Oh no," Adam thought. "She didn't tell us about this. It's not on the timetable.")

"Looking at some of the answers I've been getting lately, I can't be certain if there isn't cheating going on in this class. You all know that cheating is not allowed." She paused to look around the class.

Adam saw Josie's face go red. He thought he saw James's face go pale.

"So we are going to move two people from each table, and they will move to the table to their left. If I find matching answers between anyone sitting next to each other, I'll be suspicious. Harry and Shirin, you move to this table, James and Anita, you move here, Simon and Joe, you move here…"

Adam was relieved to find he stayed in the same place. But the noise and movement made him feel unsettled. Like everyone else, he took out his exercise book and waited for the maths quiz to start.

"Write 0.75 as a fraction."

¾, Adam wrote. The questions kept coming. At first it was easy. But then Adam began to feel like he did when they stood in a circle and practised throwing and catching. He couldn't keep up. He couldn't react quickly enough. He started to feel himself panic. What had she said? He missed the question. "That's wrong," he thought as he put down any answer he could think of.

"Right everybody. Put down your pencils, and swap books with the person sitting next to you."

Adam marked Shirin's book: $\frac{17}{20}$. To his dismay, when Shirin passed him back his own exercise book she had written $\frac{13}{20}$. Adam felt his face start to feel hot, as his eyes filled with tears. Mrs White came round each table, checking the marks and gathering up the books. She had seen Adam trying to fight back tears. As she looked down to see his score written in his book, she could see why. She glanced over at Josie's open book and saw that she had $\frac{18}{20}$. "This is going to be difficult," she thought to herself.

As she went to pick up the book in front of him, Adam grabbed it off her and burst out, "No, you can't have it. I want to take it again. It's not fair. All the noise upset me. You're not having it." His voice was getting higher and higher, and she knew from experience that this wasn't a time to try to reason with him.

"Come on, Adam. We'll go along to the quiet room."

"No, I'm not going. I want to do the quiz again," Adam was crying now and shouting.

Mrs White left the classroom assistant, Miss Foyle, in charge of the class while she took Adam down to the quiet room. She gave him a glass of water and suggested he did his breathing exercises. She counted with him, "1…2…3…4…5". Gradually she could see him calming down.

She could feel *herself* getting tense though. She knew from checking the scores as she collected the books that Josie had scored the top mark in the class. And she knew how Adam was likely to react when he learned that his closest friend had won and he hadn't. As Josie was joint winner of the hieroglyph challenge, that meant that she was now in first place in the competition. She thought it best to tell Adam here, rather than in the classroom.

When she thought he was calm enough, she started to talk to Adam about the tortoise and the hare. "Do you remember, Adam, when Mr Williams told you all the story of the Tortoise and the Hare?"

Adam looked at her, and nodded.

"Although the tortoise comes first, do you remember that Mr Williams said the story reminded us that lots of different qualities are important."

"Yes. I remember."

"Well, coming first isn't always the most important thing. Learning to deal with not coming first is probably more important. Do you understand?"

"Yes. But I wanted to win. It wasn't fair. I can't have won with $13/20$. Shirin got $17/20$. Did she win?"

"No, Adam, you didn't win. Not this time. And neither did Shirin," said Mrs White carefully. She could see that Adam was close to tears again.

"Adam, I think you like playing adventure fantasy games like Dungeons and Dragons. Am I right?"

"Yes," said Adam.

"My son is into D&D too, but I don't know very much about it."

"I could teach you if you'd like."

"Thanks for the offer, but I think I'll leave that to you young ones. From what I can gather, the characters all have certain qualities to help them with their quest. Is that right?"

"Partly."

"Well, there are certain qualities that ordinary people, like you and me, need to help us on our quest through life. Patience is one: realizing that we sometimes have to wait to achieve what we want. And courage, too, to face the things we find difficult. Another kind of courage is acceptance: accepting the way things are, and not becoming too unhappy about it."

As she said this, Mrs White was writing down the words

PATIENCE   COURAGE   ACCEPTANCE

"Look at these three words, Adam. These are important words. They are more important than the word 'winning'. Here, see if this helps you to understand and remember this." She took a piece of paper and drew a bar graph, like this:

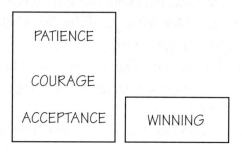

Adam looked at the drawing and asked abruptly, "Who won the maths quiz?"

Mrs White paused. "Josie," she said.

"I knew she would," shouted Adam. "I knew she'd beat me. I'm not her friend any more."

Chapter 8

Van Gogh and the Comic Strip

Eventually Adam was calm enough to go back to the classroom, to join the others for the last half hour of art. Meanwhile, as Mrs White had asked her to, Miss Foyle had given the rest of the class the results of the maths quiz.

Josie was pleased to come first, but her happiness was spoiled by knowing how Adam would react. He couldn't stand it when she beat him at anything. It was the only thing that she didn't enjoy about their friendship. She knew she wasn't very competitive compared to most people, but she did have the right to win sometimes, didn't she, without feeling bad about it?

Adam was glad the lesson was art. He enjoyed art. The art teacher, Mr Sims, came to school once a week to teach all the classes. Adam sometimes did drawing with Mrs Forest too, but that was different. Mrs Forest used drawings to go over situations that he had found difficult.

Sometimes they drew what Mrs Forest called "comic strip conversations". If there had been an upset or an argument, they would draw pictures of what had happened using drawings of stick people with speech bubbles saying what he or someone else might have said, and thought bubbles with what he and someone else might have thought. At first, he had not known what to put in other people's thought bubbles. How could he know what other people were thinking?

"That's what we're trying to help you to learn, Adam," Mrs Forest had told him. "Like lots of boys and girls with AS, you have difficulty guessing what other people are thinking and feeling." She'd said he could get clues from what a person says and the way that they say it. That's when she introduced the idea of "tones of voice".

"The expressions on people's faces can also tell you how they are feeling," Mrs Forest had told him. "But first you need to recognize expressions, and learn what they usually mean." (That's when she drew the smiley face and the face with the upside-down smile. And then showed Adam the CD-ROM.)

Mr Sims's art lesson wasn't anything to do with Mrs Forest's comic strips or smiley faces. Written up on the board were the words:

"He died young," thought Adam, doing the mental calculation without being aware that he'd done it. "He only lived to be 37. Or maybe 36."

Propped up on a table beside the board were two large books. One was open at a page with a painting of yellow flowers in a yellow vase against a yellow wall. The other book showed a man with silvery blue skin and orange hair and beard. Swirls of pale blue, green and grey covered his clothes and the background.

The other children were already painting. Mr Sims called Adam over to the board. He started explaining that paintings could do more than represent objects, or landscapes, or animals, or people.

"Or cars," said Adam.

"Or cars, Adam," smiled Mr Sims.

"What I was going to say," he continued, "is that paintings can also express feelings."

He asked Adam to look at the two paintings and say if he could see any difference in the feelings that Van Gogh might be expressing.

"This is like working with Mrs Forest," thought Adam. He didn't know what he was meant to say. He felt too tired for this.

"Look at the colours Van Gogh chose in these two paintings," Mr Sims said. "What do you see?"

"Yellow and bluey green."

"Would you say one of those colours was warm and one was cold?"

"Well, the yellow looks hot, like the sun."

"Well done, Adam," said Mr Sims. (Adam smiled with pleasure at giving the right answer.) "This painting is called *Sunflowers*. Van Gogh loved the colour yellow. Partly because it was hot like the sun. It made him happy."

"He doesn't look very happy," said Adam. "In his portrait, he's not smiling. His mouth is nearly an upside-down smile. Like in the pictures Mrs Forest does that are supposed to look unhappy."

"You're right again, Adam," smiled Mr Sims.

Adam was enjoying this now. He loved it when he got things right, especially when he was praised for it.

"When he painted this portrait, he was really very unhappy," Mr Sims continued. "And it shows in his painting, don't you think? Van Gogh didn't just paint what he saw. His paintings express how he felt. And that's what we're going to do today. I'd like you to paint your own self-portrait, choosing colours and using brush strokes that express an emotion, a feeling."

about real situations, giving him the social information he needed. His mum continued. "It's called 'How we can mend broken friendships'." She read aloud, slowly, glancing at Adam now and again.

How we can mend broken friendships

It can be nice to have friends.

"Mrs White says we're not supposed to use the word 'nice'," interrupted Adam.

"Sorry. Cross it out and put in another word if you like." She passed Adam a pen from his desk. He crossed out "nice", and wrote in "great".

"I'll start again," said Mum.

It can be ~~nice~~ **great** to have friends. Sometimes it can feel quite easy to get on with friends. But sometimes friends don't get on well. This doesn't have to be a permanent thing. It can be a temporary thing, because there are ways of mending broken friendships. Like mending broken cars, you have to think about what's gone wrong and think of ways to make things OK again.

Josie has been my friend for a long time.

"For two years and four months," said Adam. Mum smiled and stroked his hair. He didn't push her away.

We usually enjoy playing together. But we have upset each other. I felt upset and angry about Josie winning the maths quiz. This is because I wanted to win.

Because of these feelings I said unkind things to Josie. I might have made her think that I don't like her any more and that I don't want to be her friend any more. But I do.

Mum put the first sheet of paper down on the bed, so that Adam could keep looking at it if he wanted to. She began reading the second sheet.

A good way to try to make friends with someone again is to write a letter.

You could start your letter by saying sorry you upset her by saying and writing unfriendly things.

Then you could try to explain how you felt, and try to explain why.

Then you could tell her that you want to be friends with her, and write a list of the things that you like about her.

To end the letter, you could perhaps draw a picture of the two of you playing happily together.

"What do you think, Adam? Do you want to write Josie a letter?"

"I don't know."

"Do you want to be friends with Josie?"

"Yes. But she doesn't like me."

"Only because you made her think you didn't like her. I think a letter could help."

"All right."

"Good. Give us a cuddle, and come and have breakfast. After breakfast, you can write your letter, and I'll drive you round to Josie's."

Adam stood outside the front door of Josie's house, feeling very nervous. He did his breathing exercises as he waited for someone to answer the doorbell. His mum stood behind him. After what seemed like an hour, the door opened and Mrs Bell, Josie's mum, appeared.

"I've come to say sorry to Josie," said Adam abruptly.

"Hello Adam. Hello Sue," said Mrs Bell. "Come on in."

"I've written Josie a letter," said Adam, pushing it into Mrs Bell's hand as they entered the hallway.

"Well, why don't you go up and knock on Josie's bedroom door, and give her your letter, Adam. She's told me about yesterday, and she is still upset. But I expect she'll still want to see you. You go on up. Mum and I will be in the kitchen if you need us."

"Will you come with me, Mum? I'm scared."

"You'll be OK, Adam. Be brave. Some things you need to try to do on your own. I won't be far away."

And she went into the kitchen, leaving Adam at the foot of the stairs, wanting to go home, but wanting to see Josie too. He took a deep breath and started to climb the stairs.

Josie's door was open and Adam could see her sitting on her bed, reading. He stood outside the door. "I've written you a letter," he said.

Josie looked up. "Why?"

"I wanted to say I'm sorry and that I want us to be friends. Do you want to read it?"

"OK, Adam," smiled Josie. "Come in."

Without saying anything, Adam came in and handed Josie the letter. Josie opened the envelope (smiling at the drawing of a horse on the front), pulled out the piece of paper and read:

Dear Josie

I'm sorry I upset you. I felt angry with you, because I wanted to win the maths quiz. I'm good at maths. But you're good at maths too. I'm still upset that I didn't win. I shouldn't have got all those questions wrong. But I'm not angry with you any more. I want to be your friend again. I like you because you are fun to be with and you like doing the same things as me. I like playing our games together. I would be sad if we didn't play together any more.

Adam

After she read it, Josie didn't say anything. She got off the bed, and went over to her desk. Adam thought she was going to tell him to go away. He watched her as she started writing on his letter. Was she so angry she was crossing it out?

But soon, unusually for Adam, he was pleased to find out that he had made a wrong guess. Josie handed him back the letter, with two additions.

The stick figure labelled Josie now also had a speech bubble and a thought bubble. Inside the speech bubble, she had written "That's OK." Inside the thought bubble were the words "I like Adam. I want to be his friend."

Chapter 10

Riddles, Quizzes and Jigsaws

It was Monday morning. Adam looked down at the folded sheet of paper that Mrs White had handed out. He could hardly bear to wait to unfold it.

"Does everyone understand?" asked Mrs White. "As soon as you think you know the answer, put up your hand. If more than one person puts up their hand at the same time, I'll ask them to write the answer down, and when I ask them, to read it aloud. No shouting out the answer before I ask. OK? I'll count you down: 3...2...1...open."

```
               WHO AM I?

   My start is in kind but not in kin
     My ending not in out, but in
     In legends I am sometimes green
  In paintings, fighting knights I'm seen
    Beware my teeth, beware my tail
     If this riddle you should fail
    But if you win, if you be brave
   You may find treasure in my cave
```

Adam's eyes scanned the lines impatiently. "My start is in kind, but not in kin." What does that mean? He ignored the next line. It seemed to make no sense at all. He glanced down to the last line. Treasure. Cave. That's a clue, he thought. He looked back up to the top. Suddenly the first line made sense. "It's D," he realized. Then the next line seemed obvious. "It's N – there are no Ns in OUT, but there is one in IN," he thought.

Adam raised his hand quickly, almost leaping out of his seat with excitement, and looked up to make sure that Mrs White had seen him. Then he saw to his dismay that three other hands were being held up too. One of the hands belonged to Josie. The other two who had guessed the riddle were Shirin and Andrew.

"That was quick!" said Mrs White. "Now will you four write down the answer on your riddle sheet."

Adam wrote DRAGON.

"Now read out your answers," said Mrs White. "Adam, you first."

"Dragon," said Adam.

"And Josie?"

"Dragon," said Josie.

"Dragon," said Shirin and Andrew.

"Well done. Four winners for today's challenge!" said Mrs White.

"And Josie is still ahead," thought Adam.

Tuesday's challenge was a jigsaw. Mrs White divided the class into five teams of six, and each team had to complete the same jigsaw against the clock. The jigsaw was set up around the top table, so that no one else could get close enough to see the pieces until it was their turn. The team that finished quickest would win.

Adam wasn't looking forward to this challenge. He had never found jigsaws easy, though Josie said her cousin Tom was brilliant at them. So Adam was very glad to find that he was in a team with Anita, who sat next to him. Anita was great at jigsaws too. Charlie, Emma, Shirin and Douglas were also on the team, but he didn't know whether they were good at jigsaws or not. Adam's was the last team to go. The fastest team so far had completed it in 5 minutes and 34 seconds.

The pieces were all on the table, face up. The picture they were trying to make – dinosaurs in a Triassic landscape – had been stuck to the table top. Mrs White counted "3...2...1...start". Anita was off.

Adam watched her with surprise. Anita was a very quiet girl, and shy. She never usually told anyone what to do. But in this challenge, she suddenly took command. As she gathered up the four corner pieces, she gave instructions.

"Adam, you collect all the pieces with straight edges, and put them here. Charlie and Emma, you collect the blue sky pieces, and put them here. Shirin, you collect the pieces with dinosaurs on them. Douglas, you collect the grass and trees."

With clear instructions, Adam knew what to do and was soon absorbed with his task of collecting the straight pieces. As fast as he could collect them, Anita was putting them in their correct order, fitting them together to form a square frame. Adam checked the timer on the table. It read 2:40. Two minutes 40. Two minutes 54 seconds to go. Would they make it? He'd done what Anita had told him to do, and now he didn't know what to do. He sat and watched Anita as she swiftly fitted in the pieces.

"Hand me that blue piece please, Adam," said Anita, pointing. Adam handed her a piece of sky. "No, not that one. That one."

Adam handed her another piece. Wrong again. "Don't worry, I'll get it," said Anita, and leaned over to collect another piece.

"Sorry," said Adam, feeling annoyed with himself. The timer read 5:04.

"Don't worry," said Anita. "You can't be good at everything." And Anita was obviously good at this. Soon, mainly thanks to her, there were only eight pieces left to go in.

Adam looked at the timer. It read 5:14. "Oh no," thought Adam, "only 20 seconds." The seconds kept coming on the timer, 24, 25, 26. Three more pieces. 28, 29, 30.

"Finished," shouted Anita. Mrs White pressed the button on the timer. Five minutes and 31. They'd won.

"Well done, Anita," said Adam. "You were brilliant."

"Thank you," smiled Anita shyly.

Adam and Josie were now equal-first on points. At lunchtime they managed not to talk about it, but just enjoyed playing their medieval game. Josay had lost a precious bangle (an elastic band decorated with red ink jewels), and she and Damar were searching for it in the little copse of trees at the edge of the playing field. Just as they found it hanging from a low branch, the bell rang for the end of lunch.

There was no time to discuss the school challenge. Adam was relieved. He so wanted to win, but he also wanted to keep Josie as a friend. He felt pulled in two ways, and that felt confusing and uncomfortable and bad.

"You can both be friends, even if one of you wins, Adam," said Dad that evening as they all ate tea.

"Josie will be happy for you if you win," said Mum.

"Why doesn't she let me win then?" asked Adam.

"Because **she** has a right to win too," Mum replied. "One of the most important things you can learn from these challenges, Adam, is to be a good sport."

"I do want to be a good sport. But I also want to win. I want to be a champion."

"Everyone wants to win, but not everyone can. Good sports are good sports whether they win or lose. Remember that."

Adam tried to remember that the next day when he didn't win the class quiz. He usually did really well in quizzes, but this was a team quiz, and everyone on his team had to answer individual questions. The quiz team was his usual table. So at least it meant that Josie hadn't won either. Both she and Adam had answered their questions correctly, but Anita and James had got theirs wrong.

At first, Adam felt really angry with Anita. Surely she must have known that Nairobi is the capital of Kenya, not South Africa. They'd studied Kenya last year.

"Still," thought Adam, "I wouldn't have been on the winning team for the jigsaw if Anita hadn't been brilliant at that. But James should have been able to spell October by now. It's not even a difficult month, like February."

Chapter 11

The Concerns Board

At the back of Adam's class was a Concerns Board. If children had a private worry that they wanted help with, they could write the problem on a blue sticky label and stick it to the Concerns Board. Next to the Concerns Board was the Possible Solutions Board.

Anyone who had read a concern and thought they had an idea that might help could write it on a yellow label, and stick that on the Possible Solutions Board. Both Concerns and Solutions were supposed to be anonymous, and most people wrote in capitals so that their handwriting wouldn't be recognized.

That Thursday, while Adam was taking his exercise book from his tray, he glanced up at the board.

There were four Concerns:

I WANT A
HAMSTER AND
MY MUM WON'T
LET ME.

Someone had written on the Solutions Board:

GET A GUINEA
PIG

Adam thought he knew who had written the next
Concern. It said:

SOMEONE IS
CHEATING.

On the Solutions Board opposite, Mrs White had written:

Whoever wrote this, please come to the quiet room at 1.15.

The next Concern was:

MY PARENTS LIKE MY SISTER BETTER THAN ME

There were two Solution stickers:

ALL PARENTS ARE UNFAIR (SEE HAMSTER PROBLEM)

and a more constructive one:

DON'T WORRY IT JUST SEEMS LIKE THAT SOMETIMES. I EXPECT THEY REALLY LOVE YOU.

(Someone had scrawled YUK next to this.)

The last Concern was in untidy writing. It said:

scool is to

hrd

At 1.15pm, Josie and Adam stood outside the quiet room. Josie had asked Adam to come with her because she was scared. But even with Adam beside her, she was still scared. She hated the idea of telling on someone. She knocked quietly. Mrs White opened the door. "Oh dear," Josie thought. "There's no going back. I'll have to tell her now."

"I asked Adam to come with me. Is that OK?" Josie asked.

"That's OK with me," said Mrs White. "In fact, it might help. Would you excuse me just a moment. I just have to check with someone else," she said and closed the door.

"Oh dear," said Josie to Adam. "There are other people in there with her. Who do you think it is? Do you think it's Mr Williams?"

"I don't know," said Adam, thinking, "And why does my being here help?"

A few seconds later, Mrs White opened the door again. "Come in, you two," she said. "James is here already." James was sitting in the corner. His eyes were red. He was resting his chin in his hands.

"Oh no!" thought Josie. "I can't tell her James is cheating when James is here!" Her cheeks flushed red.

"Don't worry, Josie," said Mrs White gently. "James has already told me about the cheating. You don't need to worry about telling tales."

"He's also told me that he's said unkind things to you, Adam. And he's sorry about it."

"He always laughs at me if I knock things over, or if I miss a ball, or even if I do well in computers and stuff," said Adam.

"I know. He's told me. Why do you think James does that?" asked Mrs White gently.

"I don't know," replied Adam. "He takes pleasure in my mistakes. Because he's mean."

"No, James isn't mean. Just a bit unhappy," replied Mrs White gently. She turned to James. "James, would you like to tell Josie and Adam what we have just been discussing?"

James said nothing.

"Would you like me to speak for you?"

James nodded silently.

"Well. I asked James to come to see me because he'd written on the Concerns Board that he found school too hard."

"He spelt it wrong," said Adam.

"Adam!" said Josie, and gave him a "look" which he didn't understand. He realized that she was trying to give him a message with her eyes, but he couldn't tell what it meant.

"Yes, Adam. Spelling is one of the things that James finds difficult. And he feels bad about that."

"Is that why you copy mine?" Josie asked James.

James nodded.

"Oh," said Josie, and looked at the ground.

"James wants you to know that he is dyslexic. Do either of you know what that means?"

"No," they both said together.

"Well, it means that James has some difficulties with his reading and writing. He's clever, and he has lots of skills, but his dyslexia means he needs special help with the things he finds difficult."

"I need special help sometimes too. Because of my AS. But I've got lots of skills too, Mrs Forest says," said Adam.

"I know, Adam. You have. Lots of skills. Just like James. But James has been feeling bad about himself for finding schoolwork difficult and needing extra help."

"So I took it out on you two," James interrupted. "I'm sorry. At my old school, people said I was stupid. So I wanted to make it look as if I was good at spelling and stuff. And I wanted to pick on someone else, instead of being picked on. I'm sorry."

Chapter 12

An Act of Bravery

There were no challenges that day. The next day was Friday. Friday's challenge was to write a story or a poem. Adam hadn't been particularly looking forward to this. He liked writing, but he mostly liked writing lists. He loved writing lists. About cars or dinosaurs or Dungeons and Dragons characters.

As soon as ERIC was finished, Mrs White wrote on the board in big letters:

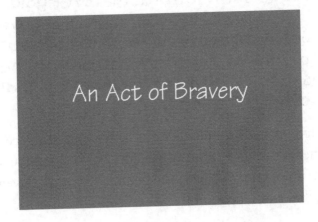

An Act of Bravery

Mrs White explained that they had 30 minutes to write a story or a poem about an act of bravery. "I'll mark them over the weekend," she said.

James and Adam looked at each other. James's nasty smile wasn't there any more. His face looked pale.

"What can I write about?" thought Adam. His mind wandered as he looked over to see if Josie had started, and suddenly found himself thinking about their medieval adventures. "That's it," he thought. "I'll write a story of one of our adventures. There are always lots of acts of bravery in them." Suddenly he wasn't worried about the story any more. And he forgot about wanting to win. He just told the story of Damar and Josay's adventures.

AN ACT OF BRAVERY

(he wrote in what he thought looked like medieval letters).

Josay was an elf princess. She had long golden hair, and wore long green robes. She had a bracelet of elf gold.

This bracelet was magical. It gave Josay bravery. Without it she was afraid of the dark, afraid of the shadows, afraid of the monsters that dwelt in the shadows.

(Adam smiled to himself as he wrote this sentence. He remembered it exactly, word for word, from the first adventure book he and Josie had looked at. He loved its rhythm and repetition.)

One morning, Josay woke up and her bracelet was gone! She looked everywhere. But it was nowhere to be found.

"Perhaps I dropped it in the dark wood," Josay said to herself. "I'm scared of the dark wood. I need Damar to help me find it. I need him to help me be brave."

She couldn't phone Damar, because this was in medieval times, and they didn't have phones then. So she sent a messenger with a message telling him to come. Damar arrived. He had his Ancient Sword of Light and Truth.

They went to the dark wood. Damar's sword lit up the dark wood, and revealed two goblins hiding behind a bush. Damar's sword made the goblins tell the truth. They told him that they had found the bracelet, and hidden it at the top of a tree, the highest tree in the dark wood.

Adam thought about who would be brave enough to climb to the top of the highest tree. Adam wanted it to be Damar – because that was **his** character. He started writing again… Damar … But then he thought again. He remembered that when he was at Josie's house at the weekend she had said that when they played their games he never wanted to give her a shot at being the hero. So now he would give Josay the chance to be brave. He crossed out the word ~~Damar~~ and continued, without stopping.

> Josay climbed the tree, even though she didn't have her bravery bracelet. It was a long climb, and she slipped a few times. But soon she was at the top. She put her bracelet on her wrist, and waved to Damar.
> "Well done Josay!" he shouted. "That was a superb act of bravery!"

Josie wondered what she would write. At first, she thought about writing about her and Adam's adventures too. Then she looked up at Adam, and saw that he had written the word Josay at the top of his sheet of paper. "I'd better choose something different," she thought. "But what?"

As she looked over at Adam, whose head was bent low over his paper, grasping his pencil really hard as he always did, an idea came. "I know, I'll write about Adam! About how brave he was to come and say sorry, and admit why he acted the way he did."

She glanced over at James. She didn't have to try to block him from copying her work now. And anyway, he wouldn't copy a story. That would be really obvious.

Thinking about James gave her another idea. How brave James had been. To admit that he'd cheated, and explain why he acted like he had – in front of Mrs White, and her and Adam. That was really brave. "I'm going to write about James and Adam," she decided. "But I won't put in their names." She picked up her pen, and started in her neat script.

An Act of Bravery

Last Saturday a friend of mine did an act of bravery. The day before, he had upset me. He had told me he hated me. He was jealous, because I had beaten him in a competition.

He never likes me beating him. I don't often beat him, but it feels good to win sometimes. I know losing makes him feel bad about himself. And I know he feels bad about himself because he's a bit different from other people. But as I keep telling him, being different is cool.

I tell him we're all different. My Mum's got a twin sister. They look alike, but they're different. Mum is very calm, but Auntie Julia is always rushing around and worried. "We may look alike," Mum says, "but we're unique, like every single person on this planet."

And that's what I tell my friend – "You're unique. Like every single person on this planet."

Anyway, I was feeling miserable. Then my friend did his act of bravery. It might not seem very brave. He just said sorry. It was like in one of our adventures. It was like I was sitting in the Cave of Sorrow (my bedroom actually) and he'd rescued me with an act of bravery.

Saying sorry is a brave thing to do. And this friend wasn't the only one who said it. Another friend said sorry. He was brave enough to say he had a problem too. My Mum says admitting we need help is one of the bravest things we can do. And she says: "We all need help. Every single person on this planet." She's wise, my Mum.

Josie put her pencil down, thought for a moment about her Mum, and how it must be hard for her to bring Josie and her sisters up without their Dad. Then she picked up her pencil again, and wrote

And brave.

James sat, wondering what to write. He thought he'd write a poem. "Less words," he thought, "and Mrs White says poems don't have to rhyme." He wrote:

an act of bravry

wen its hrd to undurstand
wen its hrd to put yor thorts on paper
u hav to be brave

wen its hrd to be difrent
Wen yor not like the rest
wen u sit at yor desk
and wunder wat to right
then comeing to scool
is an act of bravry

Chapter 12 $\frac{1}{2}$

Dear Reader

This is the author talking directly to you again. As you know, this story is about Adam's Alternative Sports Day. It also has alternative endings.

Now is the time to go and find dice, or if you don't have any, a coin.

If you throw 1, 2 or 3 with your dice, or throw "heads" with your coin, turn to page 84 and read Chapters 13a and 14a. If you throw 4, 5 or 6, or throw "tails", turn to page 98, and read Chapters 13b and 14b.

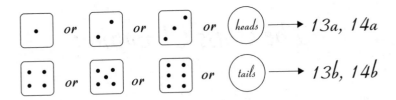

Both these endings could happen. Wanting something to happen, doesn't always make it happen, even if you do work really hard. There is always an element of chance in everyone's life. Sometimes we win, and it can feel wonderful. But sometimes, when we lose, we might actually achieve something more important. It all depends on how we respond.

Where will chance take Adam and his friends? Will Adam win or lose the Challenge Cup? And if he loses, will he gain something more important than winning? Let's see. Throw your dice, or toss your coin.

13a

The Class Champion

On Monday morning, the school playground was buzzing with excited noise, as everyone talked about who would be the class champions. Adam stood at the school gates beside Mum, watching. He never liked the early morning excitement before everyone lined up to go into school, and usually waited until the bell went before entering the playground. And this morning he felt especially flustered.

He **so** wanted to be chosen as class champion. He was pretty sure that it was between him and Josie. He hadn't been able to get to sleep until past midnight, and still woke up a few hours later from a bad dream in which he was shouting at Josie and trying to grab a silver cup from her hands.

So he was tired. Tired, but excited, and desperate to know the results. Josie arrived and stood next to him quietly. James, who was kicking a football as usual, spotted them and waved.

As soon as registration was taken, Mrs White asked the class to be silent. "I've been reading your stories and poems about An Act of Bravery, and I'd like to say how well **all** of you have done. It was really difficult to choose a winner." Everyone shifted in their chairs. "But I **have** chosen the winner."

She paused. Adam felt his chest go tight as he waited to hear. Would it be his story about Josay and Damar? He thought it was a good story.

Mrs White made her announcement. "It's James! Well done, James. It was a very moving poem. It's a very personal poem too, so I won't read it out without your permission." James, who had gone bright red, said nothing.

Adam didn't know what he felt. He was glad for his new friend. And at least it meant that Josie hadn't won the writing competition. Then he felt bad about feeling that. But he had wanted to win, because that would have made sure that he was class champion. He hated it when his feelings felt all muddled up like this. He wanted one thing, but he wanted something else too. Or he **wanted** to want something else. He took a deep breath, and tried to keep calm.

"Would you allow me to read your poem, James?" asked Mrs White.

James said nothing, then suddenly blurted out, "OK."
Josie turned to him and whispered, "Well done."
Mrs White read the poem. This is what it sounded like:

An Act of Bravery

When it's hard to understand
When it's hard to put your thoughts on paper
You have to be brave

When it's hard to be different
When you're not like the rest
When you sit at your desk
And wonder what to write
Then coming to school
Is an act of bravery.

Everyone clapped. James felt a mixture of embarrassment and pleasure. "When Mrs White is reading it out, you can't hear the spelling mistakes," he thought to himself. "It sounds good."

Adam clapped with the rest of the class. That's just how he felt most of the time, coming to school, feeling different. "We're alike, James and me," he thought. For a moment, he forgot about the championship. It was a short moment though. When the clapping stopped, Mrs White spoke again.

"And now it's time to announce the class champion. It's very close. In fact, in our class there are just three points separating the top three. I'll do this in reverse order, as they do on television!"

She picked up a piece of paper from her desk. "In third place, with 26 points is, Shirin. Well done, Shirin."

Again, everyone clapped. Shirin beamed a huge smile and blushed.

"In second place, with 27 points," said Mrs White. She paused. Adam could feel his heart beating. He stuck his fingernails in the palms of his hands, trying to block out all the confusing feelings. "In second place…is Adam. Well done, Adam."

Once more everyone clapped. Adam felt the tears building up in his eyes. But with a huge amount of effort, more than he had thought possible, he held them back and didn't burst into tears.

During the weekend, he and Mum had done a Social Story about winning and losing, about being a "good sport", and about what Mum called "putting on a brave face". Mum had told him that it was a bit like putting on a mask. You could "put on a brave face" by making an expression that made your face look as if you were feeling OK, even when you weren't. She had drawn a picture for him, as she often did when she was trying to explain things to him, and called it

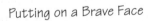

Putting on a Brave Face

How you feel   How you look

Mum said that "putting on a brave face" was a useful thing to do sometimes when you felt really disappointed, but didn't want to show it.

"Why wouldn't you want to show it?" Adam had asked.

Mum said that sometimes showing how disappointed you feel might spoil things for other people. And sometimes, Mum had told him, you might not want other people to see how upset you felt, and putting on a brave face could stop you from feeling embarrassed about feeling upset. So you could **pretend** you felt OK by putting on a brave face.

Adam didn't feel embarrassed when he was upset. He just felt upset. So he didn't really understand what Mum meant about that. But he **did** understand about spoiling things. He knew he had spoiled it for Josie when she had won the maths quiz. He knew that could have spoiled their friendship. He forced himself to put on a smile, and looked down at his desk, staring intensely at a pattern in the wood grain, trying to keep back his tears.

When he heard the next announcement, it was if someone was talking in another room, and as if it wasn't him hearing the words. "In first place, just one point ahead of Adam, is Josie. Well done, Josie. You are our class champion."

Everyone clapped. Everyone except Adam. He looked up to find Josie looking over at him. "She should look happy," he thought. "She's won. But she's not smiling."

Then, he realized. Perhaps it was like before, when she had won the maths quiz and he had spoiled it for her by being jealous and unkind. Telling himself (silently) to keep his brave face on, Adam once again forced himself to keep smiling. It was a hard thing to do, harder than the most difficult, scary challenge he had dreamed up for Damar. But he managed it.

"Well done," he said.

Josie's eyes filled with tears. "Thank you," she said quietly.

"Why is she going to cry?" thought Adam. "I thought she'd be happy."

That afternoon as usual, Adam's mum was waiting for him at the school gates. She was aware that she would know straight away whether or not he had been chosen as the champion. He didn't rush over and give her the good news, so she knew he hadn't been chosen. Yet he didn't look as upset as she thought he would be. Mrs White came out with Adam.

"I didn't get to be champion, Mum. Josie did," said Adam.

Adam's mum put her hand on his shoulder. "Oh well. Not everyone can win, and you've done really well."

"Yes, he has," said Mrs White. "He's done **really** well. He came second. There was just one point in it."

"Well **done**, Adam," said Mum.

89

"And he coped really well," continued Mrs White. "I know how difficult it was for Adam to come second, but he has obviously been working really hard on coping with disappointment."

"I put on a brave face," Adam interrupted.

"So we're very pleased with Adam," Mrs White continued. "I've had a word with the headteacher, and we've decided that Adam made such an effort to be sporting, and control his feelings and congratulate Josie that he will be awarded the Good Sport Cup this year. It will be presented at the award ceremony after the Alternative Sports Day."

Adam's mum felt so moved that she found it difficult to speak. She had allowed herself the fantasy of imagining Adam holding up the Challenge Cup. But this was better than that. This was a really **major** achievement for Adam. To cope with trying hard and nearly – but not quite – coming first was a challenge she just hadn't thought he could manage. She hugged her son tightly.

Chapter 14a

The Cup

On the morning of the Alternative Sports Day, Adam was sitting next to James at the front of the crowd in the school hall, as the seven champions prepared to take part in their challenges. Though he wished he was with them, he felt good inside, knowing that he had managed to be a good sport. And knowing he would get a cup to prove it!

The champions' first challenge was a riddle. After reminding the children in the audience not to shout out the answer even if they thought they knew it, Mr Williams read the riddle aloud through the microphone:

Two words in one am I
One is the opposite of sky
The other one, which rhymes with sleigh
Is what many like to do all day!
What am I?
Where am I?

Adam thought about the riddle. "Opposite of sky? What could that be?... Sea?... Land?... And what rhymes with sleigh that many want to do all day?... Well, when you were at school you have to work all day. But you don't want to work... What do you want to do?... I know – it's **play**, many like to play all day!"

"Can we listen to the riddle again, please?" Josie asked.

Mr Williams read out the riddle again.

"Josie's brilliant at riddles," thought Adam. "She should get this." He went back to trying to crack the riddle.

"Play... Play what?" he thought to himself. "Play Land, Play Sea? Sea Play? What was it? It could be a thing, because it said What am I? Or it could be a place, because it said Where am I?"

Suddenly the answer came to him! "Playground. Ground is the opposite of sky!" He turned to James. "I've got it," he said excitedly.

"Shh!" said James. "Don't give the game away." Then remembering that Josie had told him that Adam usually needed metaphors to be explained, he added, "I mean, don't let anyone else hear."

Adam didn't have to keep silent for long. Just at that second, Josie shouted, "Playground!"

Everyone left the hall and filed out into the playground. A pile of cardboard had been placed on a table. Mr Williams explained that this was a map that had been cut up. The seven champions had to work as a team to piece it back together again. The younger champions just stood there, but Josie and Jerome from Year 6 took charge and soon had the pieces stuck together.

The map gave clues to items that had been hidden in places throughout the school field. There were seven pieces of hidden "treasure", one for each champion, with just 5 minutes to find them. They went off in different directions, following their individual clues. Little Christina from Reception found hers straight away. It was under the table. With only 30 seconds to go, everyone apart from Josie had found their treasure.

Josie hadn't been able to follow her clues and had come back to the table to study the map again. She was looking worried.

"Go on Josie, you can do it!" shouted Adam.

Suddenly Josie's expression changed.

"I think she's cracked it," James said to Adam.

"Go on Josie," Adam shouted again.

Josie ran across the field – just 15 seconds to go. She reached the bench where she and Adam often sat and ate their snacks – 5 seconds to go. She bent down behind the bench and grabbed something. As she held it above her head, the bell rang to show the challenge was over. Just in time! Josie ran up and joined the others. Each champion held a certificate to be put up on the classroom wall, wrapped around a giant bag of golden chocolate coins to share out.

The final challenges took place in the school swimming pool. Adam loved the school swimming pool. He had learned to swim there, and was now one of the fastest swimmers in the school. And he could stay under water for ages. He loved being under the water. It was so peaceful.

The champions lined up on the side of the pool. The first challenge was an against-the-clock relay. Each champion had to swim a width (if they were under seven) or a length of the pool. The time limit was 15 minutes. All the school was seated along the length of the pool, clapping wildly. Although the little ones went very slowly, leaving Josie and Jerome with only 2 minutes and 30 seconds, they did it, with 10 seconds to spare!

Now came the grand finale. A treasure chest had been dropped to the bottom of the pool. One of the champions had to dive down, open the chest and find the treasure. The champions had to choose who was going to do this final, most difficult challenge. They were all given a piece of paper and told to write the name of the person they wanted, and pass their papers to Mr Williams.

The headteacher took the pieces of paper, and raised his hand for silence. "The vote is unanimous – well, it's six to one to be precise. Josie has been chosen to take on this final challenge. The time limit is one minute. Are you willing to do it, Josie?"

"Yes," Josie said quietly.

Adam and James craned their necks to get a better look as Josie stood on the side of the pool preparing to dive. She disappeared beneath the water. Everyone was silent. Twenty five seconds later she came up. Everyone started to clap, until they realized that she was empty handed. Josie glanced up at Adam and James.

"Come on Josie," they shouted together. "You can do it."

Josie kicked against the side of the pool and disappeared again. Adam watched the seconds tick by on the big clock on the wall – 48, 49. Where was she? Was she all right? As the clock ticked to 52 seconds, Josie's head broke the surface of the water. This time she was not empty handed. She swam to the side, and lifted her hand in the air. Dripping wet and shimmering in the light was the Challenge Cup!

The award ceremony took place that afternoon in the school hall. Parents had already arrived and were sitting in rows when the children filed in and took their seats. Adam's mum and dad were at the front of the parents' seating, holding hands. Josie's mum was sitting next to them. Adam and Josie waved and smiled as they came in.

First the certificates were awarded. One by one, dozens of children went up to receive theirs. The clapping was almost continuous. Then Mr Williams called for silence and announced that it was time to give out the cups for special achievements.

As well as the Challenge Cup, which was awarded to all seven class champions, there were five other cups this year. There was the Caring Child award, which went to Robert in Year 6. There was the Citizenship award for the child who had done most to help the running of the school. That went to Mary from Adam's class. The Computer Studies award was given to Mustapha from Year 4. The Music award went to a third year, Lila, who was brilliant on the piano. And there was the Good Sport Cup.

Mr Williams waited until the applause for Lila had died down. "As you will have noticed," he said, "we decided not to have the usual Sports Day Cup this year. That has been replaced by the Challenge Cup. But we do want to celebrate a particular kind of sporting achievement. Sportsmanship. For many of us, most of us in fact, the biggest sporting challenge is the challenge of being a good sport – win or lose. Being a good sport is a very important, very valuable achievement. I'm delighted to announce that Adam has won the Good Sport Cup this year. I'd like to invite him to come and take this award. Well done, Adam!"

Adam walked up to the stage with the clapping resounding in his ears. Smiling, he took the Good Sport Cup from Mr Williams, and shook hands. He grasped it tightly and was still smiling broadly as he sat down beside Josie. As he looked down at his own smiling face reflected in its shiny surface, he heard Josie's name announced as she was invited, along with the six other champions, to come onto the stage.

While the seven were all given their individual replicas of the Challenge Cup, he clapped loudly – which was not easy with the Good Sport Cup in one hand. Sitting beside him, James was clapping too. Adam felt as happy as he could remember being. Josie had won. He had won. And they had a new friend, James. This was definitely the best Sports Day ever.

THE END

Alternative ending follows...

The Class Champion

On Monday morning, the school playground was buzzing with excited noise as everyone talked about who would be the class champions. Adam stood at the school gates beside Mum, watching. He never liked the early morning excitement before everyone lined up to go into school, and usually waited until the bell went before entering the playground. And this morning he felt especially flustered.

He **so** wanted to be chosen as class champion. He was almost certain that it was between him and Josie. He hadn't been able to get to sleep until past midnight, and still woke up a few hours later from a bad dream in which he was shouting at Josie and trying to grab a silver cup from her hands.

So he was tired. Tired, but excited, and desperate to know the results. Josie arrived and stood next to him quietly. James, who was kicking a football as usual, spotted them and waved.

As soon as registration was taken, Mrs White, asked the class to be silent. "I've been reading your stories and poems about An Act of Bravery, and I'd like to say how well **all** of you have done. It was really difficult to choose a winner." Everyone shifted in their chairs. "But I **have** chosen the winner."

She paused. Adam felt his chest go tight as he waited to hear. Would it be his story about Josay and Damar? He thought it was a good story.

Mrs White made her announcement. "It's James! Well done, James. It was a very moving poem. It's a very personal poem too, so I won't read it out without your permission." James, who had gone bright red, said nothing.

Adam didn't know what he felt. He was glad for his new friend. And at least it meant that Josie hadn't won the writing competition. Then he felt bad about feeling that. But he had wanted to win, because that would have made sure that he was class champion. He hated it when his feelings felt all muddled up like this. He wanted one thing, but he wanted something else too. Or he **wanted** to want something else. He took a deep breath, and tried to keep calm.

"Would you allow me to read your poem, James?" asked Mrs White.

James said nothing, then suddenly blurted out, "OK."

Josie turned to him and whispered, "Well done."

Mrs White read the poem. This is what it sounded like:

An Act of Bravery

When it's hard to understand
When it's hard to put your thoughts on paper
You have to be brave

When it's hard to be different
When you're not like the rest
When you sit at your desk
And wonder what to write
Then coming to school
Is an act of bravery

Everyone clapped. James felt a mixture of embarrassment and pleasure. "When Mrs White is reading it out, you can't hear the spelling mistakes," he thought to himself. "It sounds good."

Adam clapped with the rest of the class. That's just how **he** felt most of the time, coming to school, feeling different. "We're alike, James and me," he thought. For a moment, he forgot about the championship. It was a short moment though. When the clapping stopped, Mrs White spoke again.

"And now it's time to announce the class champion. It's very close. In fact, in our class there are just three points separating the top three. I'll do this in reverse order, as they do on television!"

She picked up a piece of paper from her desk. "In third place, with 26 points is, Shirin. Well done, Shirin."

Again, everyone clapped. Shirin beamed a huge smile, and blushed.

"In second place, with 27 points," said Mrs White. She paused. Adam could feel his heart beating. He stuck his fingernails in the palms of his hands, trying to block out all the confusing feelings. "In second place...is Josie. Well done, Josie."

Once more everyone clapped. Adam looked over at a smiling Josie and clapped too. "Well done, Josie," he said.

"Is it me?" he thought. "Have I won? Maybe she hated my story, and I got no points at all for it. Maybe someone else has won." When Adam heard the next announcement, it was if someone was talking in another room, and as if it wasn't him hearing the words.

"In first place, just one point ahead of Josie, is Adam. Well done, Adam. You are our class champion."

That afternoon Mum was waiting for Adam at the school gates as usual. She was aware that she would know straight away whether or not he had been chosen as the class champion. As he rushed over to her, trailing his open rucksack behind him, his face flushed with excitement and a smile that seemed to stretch from ear to ear, she knew.

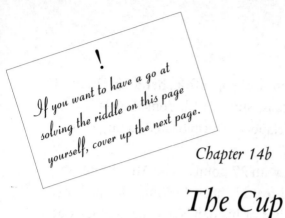

!

If you want to have a go at solving the riddle on this page yourself, cover up the next page.

Chapter 14b

The Cup

On the morning of the Alternative Sports Day, Adam was standing on the stage of the school, with the other six champions. He looked down at Josie and James, who were sitting in the front row of the audience. He had been doing his calming exercises but he still felt so excited that he could hardly stand still. He took a deep breath.

The first challenge was a riddle. After reminding the children in the audience not to shout out the answer even if they thought they knew it, Mr Williams read the riddle aloud through the microphone:

Two words in one am I
One is the opposite of sky
The other one, which rhymes with sleigh
Is what many like to do all day!
What am I?
Where am I?

Adam thought hard. "Opposite of sky? What could that be? ... Sea?... Land?... And what rhymes with sleigh that many want to do all day?... Well, when you were at school you have to work all day. But you don't want to work...What do you want to do?...I know – it's **play**, many like to play all day!"

"Any ideas?" asked Jerome, the Year 6 champion.

"I think it might be 'something play'," said Adam. No one else had any ideas to offer.

"Can we listen to the riddle again, please?" Jerome asked.

Mr Williams read out the riddle again.

"Something Play...Play Something... Play what?" Adam thought to himself. "Play Land, Play Sea? Sea Play? What was it? It could be a thing, because it said What am I? Or it could be a place, because it said Where am I?"

Suddenly the answer came to him! "Playground," he said to himself. "Ground is the opposite of sky!" "I've got it," he shouted. "Playground! It's Playground!"

"Correct!" smiled Mr Williams. "And the next clue is **in** the playground." The hall filled with the sound of applause. Then teachers, champions and audience filed outside. A pile of cardboard had been placed on a table in the centre of the playground. Mr Williams explained that this was a map that had been cut up. The seven champions had to work as a team to piece it back together again.

Adam wished Anita was with him. She was brilliant at jigsaws, but he just couldn't do them. Not knowing what to do, he watched while the others rearranged the pieces.

Soon they had the map stuck together again, and he hadn't done anything! Adam was feeling useless. Jerome could see this from his expression, and said, "Don't worry, Adam, it was you who cracked the riddle. We wouldn't have even been here if it hadn't been for you."

"Thanks," said Adam, smiling and feeling better about himself.

The map gave clues to items that had been hidden in places throughout the school field. There were seven pieces of hidden "treasure", with a different location, and a different clue for each champion, and just 5 minutes to find them. Once the champions had found their own treasure, they were allowed to help anyone else to find theirs.

Adam's clue was:

```
I have four legs and a back,
    but I cannot stand up.
I'm useful when you want to sit.
```

He stood for a few seconds, and then set off. He was sure he was right. Four legs and a back, and useful for sitting. It must be a bench. But which one? There were two benches on the school field. He ran over to the nearest bench. There was nothing there. He crouched down and looked under the seat, to see if anything had been stuck beneath it. Nothing. "It must be the other bench," thought Adam. He was feeling panicky now.

"Three minutes to go," announced Mr Williams.

Adam started to run towards the far end of the school field, to the bench where he and Josie usually sat to eat their snacks. It seemed much further away than usual, and he was out of breath when he reached it. He couldn't see anything! What was he to do?

Adam ran round to the back of the bench and there, hidden from view behind the rubbish bin, was the treasure. It was a certificate for the classroom wall and a huge bag of gold-wrapped chocolate coins to share with the class. Quickly he bent down and grabbed the treasure, then turned and ran back to the table in the centre of the playground.

Until this moment he hadn't thought of how the others were doing. He had concentrated completely on his quest to find the treasure. Now he looked around and saw five other children running across the field towards him, carrying their certificates and bags of coins. But little Christina was still standing beside the table, staring at the map.

"Are you OK?" asked Adam.

"I can't find it," said Christina. Adam noticed that her eyes had tears in them.

"I can help you," said Adam. "What's your clue?"

"One minute to go," Mr Williams announced.

"It's too late," said Christina.

"No it's not," said Adam. "Let's read the clue." He looked at the map and read Christina's clue:

```
Find me please, if you are able.
        Look beneath.
     I rhyme with stable.
```

In an instant, he had cracked it. "Bend down, Christina, and look under the tabletop," he said urgently. The others arrived back at the table, just as Christina crawled under it. A few seconds later, she crawled out, and stood up smiling with the certificate and the bag of golden coins in her hand.

"Time's up," announced Mr Williams.

"Thank you, Adam," Christina said.

"That's OK, Christina," Adam replied, feeling quietly pleased, and good about himself.

The final challenges took place in the school swimming pool. Adam loved the school swimming pool. He had learned to swim there, and was now one of the fastest swimmers in the school. And he could stay under water for ages. He loved being under the water. It was so peaceful.

The champions lined up on the side of the pool. The first challenge was an against-the-clock relay. Each champion had to swim a width (if they were under seven) or a length of the pool. The time limit was 15 minutes. All the school was seated along the length of the pool, clapping wildly. The little ones went very slowly, leaving Adam and Jerome with only 2 minutes and 30 seconds between them, but they did it, with 10 seconds to spare!

Now came the grand finale. A treasure chest had been dropped to the bottom of the pool, and one of the champions had to dive down, open the chest and take out the treasure. The champions had to choose who was going to do this final, most difficult challenge. They were all given a piece of paper and told to write the name of the person they wanted, and pass their papers to Mr Williams.

Adam desperately wanted to do the challenge himself, and was tempted to write his own name. But he knew it was against the rules to vote for yourself, so he wrote

JEROME

The headteacher took the pieces of paper, and raised his hand for silence. "The vote is unanimous – well, it's six to one to be precise."

"Will it be me or Jerome?" wondered Adam, hardly daring to listen to the result.

"I think everyone has seen how strong a swimmer Adam is. He has been chosen to take on this final challenge. The time limit is one minute. Are you willing to do it, Adam?"

Adam's heart was beating fast. "Yes," he said quietly.

Josie and James craned their necks to get a better look as Adam stood on the side of the pool, adjusting his goggles, preparing to dive. He took a deep breath, dived, and disappeared beneath the water.

As he slid beneath the surface, the familiar, comforting silence enveloped Adam. He swam deeper, pulling his arms through the water. He could see the treasure chest. In a few seconds, he would get there. Everything seemed to be going in slow motion. The chest was held shut by two padlocks, but Adam could see no key. He held on to the side of the chest and looked carefully. How would he unlock the chest with no key?

Just then he noticed that the padlocks weren't pushed into their locked position. He just had to twist them open and remove them. He grabbed the first one, and soon had the lock removed. But he needed to breathe! He tried to remove the other lock, but he needed air urgently. He felt as if his lungs would explode if he stayed under any longer. But would he have time to get to the surface and back again? There was no time to think. With a huge kick of his legs, he rose to the surface, took a deep breath, then kicked the side of the pool and swam down again.

At the pool side, Josie and James, along with everyone else, were looking at the clock anxiously – 35 seconds had ticked away.

Back beneath the water, Adam reached the chest and tried to remove the lock. But something seemed to be stopping him. He couldn't get it off. "What can I do?" he thought. He was starting to panic. Just then, the padlock twisted in his hand and came away from the catch. He'd done it!

Grabbing the handle, he lifted the lid and looked inside. There, glistening silver in the blue water, was the Challenge Cup!

As the clock ticked to 55 seconds, Adam's head broke the surface of the water. The underwater silence was replaced by the noise of more than a hundred pairs of hands clapping. Adam swam to the side and lifted his hand in the air. In his fist, dripping wet and shimmering in the light, was the Challenge Cup!

The award ceremony took place that afternoon in the school hall. Parents had already arrived and were sitting in rows when the children filed in and took their seats. Adam's mum and dad were at the front of the parents' seating, holding hands. Josie's mum was sitting next to them. Adam and Josie waved and smiled as they came in.

First the certificates were awarded. One by one, dozens of children went up to receive theirs. The clapping was almost continuous. Then Mr Williams announced that it was time to give out the cups for special achievements.

As well as the Challenge Cup, which was awarded to all seven class champions, there were five other cups this year. There was the Caring Child award, which went to Robert in Year 6. There was the Citizenship award for the child who had done most to help the running of the school. That went to Mary from Adam's class. The Computer Studies award was given to Mustapha from

Year 4. The Music award went to a third year, Lila, who was brilliant on the piano. And there was the Good Sport Cup.

Mr Williams waited until the applause for Lila had died down. "As you will have noticed," he said, "we decided not to have the usual Sports Day Cup this year. That has been replaced by the Challenge Cup. But we do want to celebrate a particular kind of sporting achievement. Sportsmanship. For many of us, most of us in fact, the biggest sporting challenge is the challenge of being a good sport – win or lose. Being a good sport is a very important, very valuable achievement. I'm delighted to announce that Josie has won the Good Sport Cup this year. I'd like to invite her to come and take this award. Well done Josie!"

Adam patted Josie on the back as she rose from her seat, and went to receive her prize.

Finally, it was time to receive the Challenge Cup. Adam and the other class champions walked up to the stage, with the clapping resounding in their ears. The Challenge Cup itself was to be inscribed with their names and kept in school. So each of the champions was presented with a replica to keep.

Adam took his Cup from Mr Williams and clasped it tightly as he stood still while Mrs White took the group photograph. Still standing on stage, he looked down at Josie and James, who were clapping wildly in the front row. He looked over to where Mum, Dad, and Josie's mum were sitting. They were clapping just as wildly. Adam smiled a deeply contented smile. He felt as happy as he could remember being. Josie had won her Cup. He had won the Challenge Cup. And they had a new friend, James. This was definitely the best Sports Day ever.

THE END

Further Reading

Other books available from Jessica Kingsley Publishers:

Fiction

Blue Bottle Mystery: An Asperger Adventure
  by Kathy Hoopmann

Of Mice and Aliens: An Asperger Adventure
  by Kathy Hoopmann

Lisa and the Lacemaker: An Asperger Adventure
  by Kathy Hoopmann

Non-fiction

My Social Stories Book
  by Carol Gray and Abbie Leigh White

Both these fascinating books are written by boys with AS:

Asperger Syndrome, the Universe and Everything
  by Kenneth Hall

Freaks, Geeks and Asperger Syndrome: A User Guide to Adolescence
  by Luke Jackson

"What emotion?" asked Adam, beginning to feel panicky. What did Mr Sims expect him to do?

"Whatever you like, Adam. Choose one from the list, or paint the emotion that you are feeling now."

As Adam sat down opposite Josie to paint his picture, his angry, resentful feelings came back strongly.

"That's horrible," he said to her, pointing to her painting. "It's a horrible picture. Mine will be better than yours."

Josie looked up at Adam, as he began to paint. She said nothing, but her face grew red with a mixture of embarrassment and hurt. Adam didn't notice. "What a strange idea," he was thinking to himself. "Painting feelings. I didn't know you could do that."

But as he began to paint, he dipped his brush into the black paint, and drew a heavy outline of his face. Before he coloured in the face, he made thick black zigzags over the background. Then he dipped another brush in red and painted in the face in bright red. It looked like an angry picture. It felt right. He didn't know why, but it felt right. Adam felt angry. The picture felt angry. He noticed a gap on the paper, which he'd accidentally left uncovered by zigzags. He picked up a pencil, and drew a thought bubble. Inside the bubble, he wrote the words "I hate Josie".

Just as he did so, Josie looked up and read what he'd written. She looked at Adam and burst into tears.

"What's the matter, Josie?" Adam asked.

Chapter 9

Saying Sorry

It was Saturday morning. Adam lay in bed feeling miserable. He'd really upset Josie and he didn't know what to do about it. He wanted to be friends again. But how?

Adam's mum and dad were in the kitchen, reading the home–school diary again. Mrs White had written:

June 6

Adam had some difficulties coping with the results of the maths quiz. He was disappointed in his own performance, which was not to his usual high standard. He became very distressed, and was taken to the quiet room to calm down. He was also upset to learn that his best friend had won the quiz. He in turn, upset her. Perhaps you could talk to Adam about this over the weekend. Mr Williams will give you a ring on Monday morning to discuss it. I hope things go well.

Mum brought Adam his cup of tea in bed. As she opened his bedroom door, he pulled the duvet over his head so that she couldn't see him. And he couldn't see her. He didn't want to see anybody.

Mum put the teacup down on the bedside table. "How are you feeling, Adam?"

"I don't want a cup of tea. I'd like to be private, please."

"Well, I'll leave your tea on the table, shall I? You drink it on your own and then come and join us in the kitchen."

"I don't want breakfast."

"What's the matter?"

No response.

"Is it Josie?"

She could see the duvet move slightly and reached over to where she thought Adam's head was, in an attempt to find his hair and stroke it.

"Go away."

She withdrew her hand.

"I'm horrible."

"No you're not, Adam. You're a kind boy."

"I was horrible to Josie."

"That doesn't mean you're horrible. It just means you made a mistake and did something horrible. We all do things we wish we hadn't." She paused. No response. "It doesn't mean we're horrible people. Not if we're sorry for what we've done. It's not the end of the world."

"What do you mean?"

"I mean it's not as bad as you might think it is. Things can be made better again."

"Don't say things I don't understand," Adam snapped angrily. Forgetting about covering himself with the duvet, he sat up in bed.

"Well, it's a metaphor," his mum explained. "We've talked about metaphors. Do you remember? Sometimes a metaphor like 'it's not the end of the world' is the best way of saying something. And you **do** understand it once it's been explained to you. Anyway, as I said, things can be made better again."

"No they can't. I told Josie I hated her. I said nasty things about her drawing. I put a horrible message in my picture. We're not friends any more."

"Would you like to make things better? Would you like to be friends again?"

"Yes," said Adam, sullenly.

"Well, would you like to have a look at something Dad and I have written to help you?"

No response.

"It's to help you understand why you behaved in that way, and how your behaviour made Josie feel. And it's to help you to put things right again."

No response.

"Can I sit next to you so we can read it together?"

"All right."

Mum moved up to sit next to Adam. "It's a kind of Social Story," she said.

Adam was used to his mum and sometimes his teachers helping him to understand social situations or prepare him for new experiences with Social Stories. They weren't stories like *The Hobbit* or *Harry Potter*, but were writings